Puny Pete The Prairie Dog

Illustrations By Maggie Curran

Karen Gehan

I am so glad I have met you!

To Dominic,
keep reading
and always be
curious!
Love,
Mrs. Gehan

Visit our website at www.StillwaterPress.com for more information.

First Stillwater River Publications Edition

ISBN-10: 1-946-30086-1
ISBN-13: 978-1-946300-86-7

Library of Congress Control Number 2018962242

1 2 3 4 5 6 7 8 9 10
Written by Karen Gehan
Illustrated by Maggie Curran
Cover Design by Kody Lavature

Published by Stillwater River Publications, Pawtucket, RI, USA.

Publisher's Cataloging-In-Publication Data
(Prepared by The Donohue Group, Inc.)

Names: Gehan, Karen, author. | Curran, Maggie, illustrator.
Title: Puny Pete the prairie dog / Karen Gehan ; illustrations by Maggie Curran.
Description: First Stillwater River Publications edition. | Pawtucket, RI, USA : Stillwater River Publications, [2018] | Interest age level: 005-009. | Summary: "Puny Pete wants to help his family 'just like his brothers and sister,' but they lovingly pat his head and tickle his tummy and tell him he's too little. Puny leaves home to prove he is 'Big.' Oh, what dangers lurked everywhere he went! Did he get hurt? Who tried to eat him? Will he ever find home again?"--Provided by publisher.
Identifiers: ISBN 9781946300867 | ISBN 1946300861
Subjects: LCSH: Prairie dogs--Juvenile fiction. | Helping behavior--Juvenile fiction. | Families--Juvenile fiction. | Autonomy (Psychology)--Juvenile fiction. | CYAC: Prairie dogs--Fiction. | Helpfulness--Fiction. | Families--Fiction.
Classification: LCC PZ7.1.G43 Pu 2018 | DDC [E]--dc23

Dedication

*To my Mom and Dad
and that Cadillac Hearse trip across the USA*

Puny Pete, the prairie dog, has a very loving family consisting of three brothers, one sister, a mom, a dad, grandparents and lots of aunts, uncles, and cousins. He was born in the same litter as his brothers and sister but all of them were fourteen inches long and weighed a whole three pounds. Puny Pete was only twelve inches long and only weighed two pounds, so they called him Puny Pete. They patted him on his head and tickled his tummy while they lovingly teased him by calling him Puny Pete.

When he wanted to "stand guard" at the top of his burrow,* his mom and dad wheezed, "Not now, but maybe when you're a little older." When he wanted to help forage* for food, his brothers and sister chirped, "You're too little. Maybe when you're bigger."

"I want to be BIG just like them," he said to himself. "I'm tired of being Puny Pete. I WANT TO BE BIG!" "Aha!"

Just then Puny Pete had an idea. "I'll prove to them that I'm BIG, just like them. I'll take a long trip to prove that I can take care of myself! So there!" Of course, he had no idea where he was going or of the dangers that lurked outside of his coterie.* He just knew that he was going to start walking and NO ONE was going to stop him!

That afternoon, while everyone was busy doing their chores he found a sagebrush* stick. He took his mother's red handkerchief from her dresser, plopped a few seeds from the larder* into it for his dinner, tied it onto the end of his sagebrush stick, and burrowed his way into the open plains.

"I'm taking a walk," he barked to his brothers.

"Bye Puny," they wheezed back.

"I'm taking a walk," he yipped to his sister when he saw her.

"Bye Puny," she chirped.

"I'm taking a walk," he yelled to his cousins, mom, and dad.

"Bye Puny," they answered. "Don't be late for dinner," chattered his mom. And before he left, his brothers and sister patted his head and tickled his tummy.

He began walking and walking and walking. After a very long time, about one whole hour, he was walking forward but looking backwards toward the home he left when BUMP!' He tripped and toppled over. He heard a screechy 'brahhh!' as a great big startled hawk flapped its gigantic black wings into the blue sky. And then... "hissss!"

"Who are you?" wheezed Puny Pete.

"Who am I?' hissed Raymond the Rattlesnake. "Who are YOU?"

"I'm Puny Pete and I want to be BIG like my brothers and sister you understand."

"Yesssss," said Raymond the Rattlesnake not understanding Puny Pete at all.

"What do you do?" chirped Puny Pete.

"I eat prairie dogssss," hissed Raymond. "However, sssssince I just ate five micccccce I'm not very hungry right now sssso I won't eat you. Besidessss, my tail hurtsss. That hawk chomped it into nearly two pieccccccesss."

"What part of your tail?" asked Puny. For now he was just a little scared. To him, all of Raymond looked like a tail.

"My rattle," replied Raymond and he rattled it as loudly as he could with the end flopping around.

"I wish I had a rattle," said Puny Pete. "Does it make you BIG?"

"I don't know if it makesss me big, but it makes a nicccce loud rattly sssound," and he shook it fiercely again, at least as fiercely as he could to be impressive.

"I'll tell you what," said Raymond. "Sssssince you sssaved my life from that hawk who wassss about to eat me, I'll let you have half my rattle ssssssince it hurtssss and issss about to fall off. But if I sssssee you again I jusssst might eat you."

"Wow!" chirped Puny Pete. "Thanks!, for the rattle part that is, not the eating part," wheezed Puny.

"Pull it off quick before I jusssst change my mind," hissed Raymond. So Puny Pete grabbed the rattle and pulled as hard as he could using his front paw claws, when THUD off it popped, with Puny tumbling head over claws away. A half mile later he sat down for a rest next to some wheatgrass.* He plucked two strands, threaded them around the rattle, and placed his new beautiful necklace around his brown furry neck. He was so proud.

After his rest he resumed his journey. It was awfully hot and he was very thirsty. Just then he saw a big white tub right next to a big red barn. "Hmm," he thought to himself. "That smells like water." Prairie dogs have a great sense of smell. He climbed up onto the ridge and balancing his rotund* little body, he dipped his head in for a nice cool drink when PLOP! in he splashed. He scrambled out looking like a drowned rat. He was shaking himself while not looking where he was going when BAM! he hit the side of a big red barn so loudly that it shook. His rattle rattled a very loud rattly sound that echoed between the barn roof rafters.

"Ssssss, Ssssss, sssssss." "Brock, brock brock. Brock, brock brock." "Cluck cluck cluck. Cluck cluck cluck." And then "ERERERRR!" There was all this noisy commotion of activity as a flurry of chicken feathers and a yellow ball of fur all rolled in a big blur blew past Puny straight out the big red barn door.

"Hurray, hurray. You save the day!" Within seconds, he was surrounded by fifty hens and a rooster. They clucked and crowed and performed their chicken dance, as only chickens can do, around and around Puny Pete. Robby the Rooster, wanting to dim the chaos, ER-ERRED and all quieted down.

"Who and What, exactly, are you?" er-erred Robby.

"I'm Puny Pete the Prairie Dog," said Puny.

"Well, you look more like a drowned rat and WE don't like rats, drowned or not! Are you sure you're not a rat?"

"I don't know what a drowned rat is but I know I'm a prairie dog," chirped Puny.

"Well, that's okay then," er-erred Robby. "You might be a prairie dog but today you are our hero, right everyone?" There was an assent as all clucked and er-erred. Robby continued, "That bobcat was going to eat us fine feathered folk and your rattle was rattly enough that he blew on by. So, In your honor, I would like to present you with half of my beautiful royal red comb. You see, in the hustle and tussle with that big tabby, his claw cut my crown in half and now I am beginning to get a terrible headache. It would help me greatly if you would pull off the broken piece with your strong front claws." So Puny pulled and pulled and pulled. Finally, SPLAT! off it came with Puny landing flat on his back.

"Oh, I feel sooo much better," er-erred Robby, "and now I present you with one-half of my official royal red crown."

"Thank you," chattered Puny. "Will it make me big?" asked Puny as the chickens tied it onto his head with a piece of twine. "Because I want to be big like my brothers and sister, you see."

"I don't know if it will make you big, but it will make you look royal," crowed Robby, who didn't see at all.

"Will you dine with us?" the chickens clucked.

"Oh, no, thank you," said Puny Pete. "I have to get big."

"Well, we will fill your handkerchief with some fine chicken grain." And they did.

Puny Pete, adorned with his rattle necklace and his royal red crown, picked up his sagebrush stick with his red handkerchief filled with chicken grain, chattered his 'thanks again' and 'good byes' and continued on his way.

It was very late in the afternoon by now and Puny Pete was getting tired. He began to miss his brothers and sister. Night was coming. His comfy bed was so far away. "Maybe I should try to find home," he thought and he almost began to cry. Hanging his head and feeling despondent, he wasn't looking where he was walking and TRIP!

"Ouch!" he yipped as he toppled over and over as his rattle rattled. "Aroo! Arooo!" *Swish*! The air from a gray fur ball whished by Puny faster than he could stand upright. "Whew, WHAT was THAT?" he chattered to himself, or so he thought.

"That was Coney the Coyote," grunted a grey striped armadillo. "You could say you're sorry, but thanks. You saved my life."

Puny jumped. "Who are you? And how'd I save your life?" wheezed Puny.

"That coyote was about to devour* me for dinner, but your rattle and crown scared him away. I'm Aaron the Armadillo. I am pleased to make your acquaintance, but to whom am I acquainting myself with, for I've never seen a creature looking quite like yourself?"

"I'm Puny Pete the Prairie Dog. I'm a long way from home and I want to be BIG like my brothers and sister, you know."

"Oh, of course," grunted Aaron the Armadillo, not knowing what he meant at all. "Oooh, my hind end hurts. Coney just sunk his teeth into my armor and nearly tore off my entire coat of arms when you came to my rescue. Actually, it is my second coat."

"Your second coat? You have two? I don't have any like yours, so one would be fine with me. I wish I had armor," Puny barked. "I think it looks cool!"

"I'll tell you what," grunted Aaron. "I've been lugging around my great grandmother's armor for twenty years and its getting to be too heavy for me. It's been on my back for so long that its sort of stuck. Since Coney already pulled off the top corner, I would much appreciate it if you could pull it off the rest of the way, but do it fast so it won't hurt so much. I've got to get it off my back."

Puny Pete sunk his teeth under the loosened part of Aaron's shield and he pulled and pulled and pulled. Finally, POP! off it came, tail and all. Puny catapulted* high into the air and THUMP down he fell into some soft thistle* landing with the armor on top of him.

He climbed out of the thistle patch clutching his prized new suit of armor and barked his thanks. "Will it make me big?"

"I'm not sure it will make you big, but it will make you look great," grunted Aaron approvingly.

"Thanks again," chirped Puny as he resumed his journey. Shortly, he began to feel very weary, for now he was wearing his rattle necklace and his royal red crown, carrying his sagebrush stick with his mother's red handkerchief, and all the while dragging his shield with an armored tail. When he saw a patch of wheatgrass, he thankfully sat down and pondered how to best carry his new armor. An idea popped into his head. "If Aaron can WEAR his shield, why can't I?" He looked around. Then he REALLY looked. "Wheatgrass!" he thought. He plucked two strands, lifted the armor onto his back and tied the strands around the armor into a big green bow right across his chest. He was so proud.

Once again, he set off on his journey. But now it was very dark. He was lonely and beginning to feel scared. "I don't want to be big anymore" he thought. "I just want to be home." He started to walk very slowly. He was soooo tired. "Yaaawn! I think I'll just take a little nap. Yaaawn."

He stretched out under a patch of purple thistle with a perfectly soft purple thistle flower pillow and fell fast asleep. He began to dream. At first it was a sweet dream. His brothers and sister were patting his head and tickling his tummy. But then he heard "Who? Who?" Then "Hisss, hisss, hisss." He mumbled, "go away."

"Hey where are my brothers and sisters?" he wondered in his dream-like state. Then he felt them tickling him again. He smiled lazily to himself.

Then it was louder, "WHO? WHO? WHO?" and "HISS HISS HISS." He woke up with a bark and a start at the same time that he rolled right over a log. "WHO? WHO? WHO?" 'FLAP! FLAP! FLAP!' As Puny toppled over, his royal red crown fell askew, his rattle rattled very loudly, and his armored tail got stuck under a log. "A log?" thought Puny. "I've never seen a log around…"

Out of the dark he heard, "Hey sssson get off my back, would ya? You're hurting me with that tail." Puny struggled to the left. He struggled to the right. He wiggled and waggled and finally SPLAT! he shot straight off the log and FUFF! landed on his back. He shook himself, which meant of course that his rattle rattled some more. He straightened out his red royal crown, and he readjusted his coat of armor with its big green bow. He picked up his sagebrush stick with the red handkerchief and barked, very grumpily, "Who are you and why did you wake me up? I was having such a pleasant dream when you woke me up!"

"I'm Dadalusssss, the diamondback rattlesnake. I didn't wake you up. That was Odie Owl. He wasssss about to eat me for his night sssssnack. Who are you?"

'I'm Puny Pete and I want to be big like my brothers and sister as you might have guessed."

Dadalus hissssed, "But of courssssse." But he couldn't, nor wouldn't, ever have guessed at all. Nor did he have any idea what Puny was talking about.

"What do you normally do?" barked Puny, not in a good mood.

"I eat prairie dogssss," hissed Dadalus. "Sssssinccccccee I jussst ate ten delicccccioussss eggsss I'm not hungry enough to eat you thisssss evening. Bessssssidessss," he said warily, "I've never ssseen a prairie dog with a rattlesssnake rattle, red crown, or a grey coat of armor and you sssseem to have all three. Are you sure you are a prairie dog?"

"Of course I'm sure I'm a prairie dog!," barked Puny. He was so tired he forgot to be insulted. Every time Dadalus hissed, he seemed to show a long curved white thing in his mouth.

"What's that white thing in your mouth?" chirped Puny?

"lt'ssss my fang.* I shoot poisssson through it to paralyssse my dinner," he said as he gave Puny a suspiciously menacing look.

"OOOeee," chirped Puny. I wish I had a fang. I've never had one of those before."

"Well," said Dadalus, "Mosssst of ussss diamondbackssss only have two; however, I am rather sssspecial much like yourssself isss looking at the moment, and happen to have three. Becausssse vou sssssaved my life from Mr. Odie Owl, I'll let you have my third fang. I've had a very bad fang-ache lately. You would be doing me a great favor if you could pull it out. Itsssss thissss one," and as he opened his mouth he portayed a rather sinister grin. Right there in the very front of his mouth was his odd third tooth. So Puny Pete pulled off a very thorny thistly branch, anchored a thorn right under that sore tooth, tied the other end to the stalk, and yipped as loudly as he could, "OOOEEE!" All the while that rattle rattled! Dadalus, the diamondback was so scared that he jerked his head back! "PLECK!" the fang flew out of his mouth and landed right on top of Puny's royal red crown.

"Thanks Puny. Itssss yourssss. Ssssssso long. Don't let a sssnake ssssneak up on you. It might be me." And he slithered away to his home in the ground.

Puny pulled the fang off his crown and sat down to study it a little more closely. "Hm, what can I do with this?" he thought. He turned it over and over. He put it into his mouth but it wouldn't fit. He held it up to the moon as he peered through it. He could see the big milky oval moon right through the hole in the white tooth. Just as he was lowering the tooth from eye level, "Aaaachoooo! " He sneezed. 'Achoo! Achoo!' echoed right through the fang off the thistle tree and back again to Puny's ears. "OOOee," he thought. "A horn! I have a horn. I've never had one of those before," he chirped as he rubbed his ears.

He settled himself once more for the night. He now had a plan. He decided to go home tomorrow. He decided to be Puny Pete. He decided he loved his brothers and sister. He decided that he loved having his brothers and sister pat his head and tickle his tummy. He decided that he liked being his very own size. "Yes," he thought, "I'm going home tomorrow."

The next morning, with his beautiful royal red crown sitting regally on his head, his rattlesnake rattle proudly rattling around his furry neck, his coat of armor snugly tied across his back with a great big green bow tied under his chin, and his white diamondback snake curled fang in one hand, and his sagebrush stick with his mother's empty red handkerchief on the end (for he had eaten every last grain of seed he had), he set off for his beloved home.

He walked and he walked. It seemed like forever but it was really only three miles. He was so lost and almost ready to give up ever finding his home when SWOOSH! SWOOSH! He looked up as he walked backwards only to see gigantic black wings. "BOOM!" Down he fell. Down, down, down a very long hole. "BAM!" He hit his bottom so hard that his royal red crown fell sideways covering one eye making him look like a fierce pirate. His rattle rattled louder than ever before and his armored tail struck a very soft creature.

Freddy the black-footed ferret was about to attack three boy prairie dogs and one girl prairie dog. Puny was so startled himself that he chattered the loudest chatter he could as he struggled to his feet. He wiggled and waggled and flung his shoulder so hard that he flipped that ferret right out of the hole with his new armored tail. He recognized his loving family and was so happy, he raised his white fang and yipped "YAY, YAY, YAY! I'M HOME!!!" which echoed off every sage brush for five miles. He scurried to his family as they huddled together even closer and yipped and barked with fear. Their eyes were huge. Their mouths were agape.

Puny stopped dead in his tracks. He almost began to cry as he wheezed, "Don't you know me? I'm your brother." No one moved. It was so still you could hear a seed drop.

"Oh, I know!" Puny yipped as his family huddled even closer together in the farthest corner of their burrow. Puny untied his royal red crown. He shed his shield with his armored tail. He removed the rattlesnake rattle. He flung the cobra fang onto the floor and barked, "NOW DO YOU KNOW ME?"
All of a sudden there was yipping, chirping, wheezing, and chattering as his three brothers, sister, mother and father hugged him and picked him up and carried him like a king around the room. They chattered "You saved the day! You saved us from Freddy the black-footed ferret!"

"RuRuRu," barked one brother to make his speech. "Puny Pete, you are now no longer Puny Pete, but PETE!" And he put out his hand for a Puny Pete to shake.

Puny Pete looked so forlorn. He hung his head. His mouth began to quiver.

"What's wrong Pete?" they asked.

"I don't want to be PETE!" he yipped. "I want to be me. I want to be Puny Pete just like always!" And so, they patted his head and tickled his tummy and barked in unison, "We missed
you Puny Pete!

Glossary

Burrow - a hole in the ground made by animals to create a living space.

Catapult - to launch something into the air.

Coterie - a small group of people or animals that have common interests.

Devour - to eat rapidly.

Fang - a large sharp tooth. The snake uses it to inject poison into its prey, the food that it wants to eat.

Forage - to search for food.

Larder - a room or cupboard used to store food.

Rotund - round and plump.

Sagebrush - a shrub that grows in North America. It is of the daisy family and grows in semiarid regions.

Thistle - a soft flowering plant with sharp prickles on the stems and leaves.

Wheat Grass - freshly sprouted first leaves of the common wheat plant.

About Prairie Dogs

The prairie dog was named "little dog" by the explorer Francois Verendrye in 1742. It is a member of the Sciuridae family, which includes ground squirrels, tree squirrels, marmots, flying squirrels, and chipmunks. Five species of prairie dogs live on the North American plains. The black-tailed prairie dogs, when full grown are between 14 and 17 inches long and weigh 1 to 3 pounds. They live from the Trans-Pecos region of Texas north through southern and eastern New Mexico, and from the Texas Panhandle to parts of North Dakota, as well as Montana, and parts of Southern Canada. They are very social animals. They eat grasses, forbs, insects, such as grasshoppers, prickly pear cactus pads, thistles, plant roots, wheat grass, gramas, and buffalo grass. Dominance among the prairie dogs is associated with their weight. The more a prairie dog weighs, the more dominant it is.

This information and more can be found in the following text:
Graves, Russell A.. *The Prairie Dog Sentinel of the Plains*. Texas Tech University, 2001.

Book Discussion Questions

1. Who are the main characters in *Puny Pete the Prairie Dog*?

2. In the beginning of the story why did Puny want to leave home?

3. List two animals that Puny met that might have eaten him if they were not hungry.

4. List an animal that Puny helped and describe how he helped that animal.

5. Of all the gifts Puny received, which is your favorite and why?

6. What is a coterie?

7. In the beginning of the story Puny Pete wanted to be big. At the end of the story, he cried because he wanted to be "Puny Pete." Why? What changed?

8. Draw a picture of your favorite part of the story.

9. What can you do now that maybe was difficult for you a year ago?

10. Who is special to you in your life?

About the Author

Karen Gehan has a master's degree in communication disorders and 6th year degree in literacy: remedial reading and language arts. She has worked a a speech language pathologist for over 30 years. She currently resides in Stonington, CT. This is her first children's book.

About the Illustrator

Maggie Curran is a mother of 8 and a grandmother of 16 wonderful grandchildren. Maggie doodles just for fun. This is her first illustrated published book. She and her husband reside in Danbury, CT.

CPSIA information can be obtained at www.ICGtesting.com
Printed in the USA
BVIW121521090119
537370BV00001B/3